AGAINST
THE ODDS

A SHORT STORY BY FELICIA GUY-LYNCH

Dedication

To all those striving
to maintain salvation

Praise for *Against the Odds*

"I love how Isaiah grew and changed into a better man (regardless of his setbacks)"
- Candace Shepherd

"If you're an adult, as old as I am or maybe older; when reading that story, you will be transported back to your childhood. If you're younger, you'll be able to identify with various situations that this young man faces. FINDING ISAIAH is this coming-of-age story that gives you a break from your reality and allows you to enter a new one. She is one of the most talented women I have had the chance to encounter. To not only take on a series of novels, but to take on this particular project and do it in the voice of a young man at that says a lot about her as a writer."
- Robert Mulolo

Preface

This book is the third short story to the *Finding Isaiah* series. The story will shift back to the standpoint of Isaiah to demonstrate his growth, restraint and resilience. He truly becomes a man of his own kind.

It is my pleasure to bring you *Against the Odds*. I hope you thoroughly enjoy.

Sincerely,

Felicia Guy-Lynch

Chapter 1

I didn't go back to school until September 2009. I wanted to go in January but we had to bury Jafari in November. I needed time to grieve and two months was too soon to be thinking about going back. When I did go back, I managed to graduate in June 2010. I remember feeling so free.

Thankfully, regardless of the 2008 recession, I managed to open up a barbershop with the help of Mom. Business was slow at first, like most start-ups. Within a couple of months, business started to pick up. Word of mouth is all the marketing I need for my business to grow.

I got a business letter together and managed to get a pretty decent amount of grants and loans. Plus, I would be creating jobs for the youth to keep them occupied and, most importantly, out of trouble.

"I'm so proud of you!" Naomi screamed in excitement.

"I couldn't have done it without you. Your loyalty is rare. I'm getting ready to move out soon." I said. "Never change."

"Only for the better," she said.

We moved in together to live in the Marylyn Monroe condos in Mississauga. I liked them so much that I got me a nice bachelor's apartment with a beautiful view. Naomi helped to decorate the new place. She was done within two weeks. Nice and swift.

Although I seem to have had everything a man could ask for, I was really missing Dad and Jafari. I wish Dad and I ended off on better terms but I couldn't have a healthy relationship with him. He had way too much pride. He was too proud to admit he messed up, went back on his word and ruined a good marriage with Mom. I know he had his reasons for doing what he did but it would have been better for him to divorce her. At least that would be the better way of going about things. If Naomi did that to me, I wouldn't be so quick to be with another woman. There's no replacing what we went through. For better or for worse are the vows and it's the hard times that truly test the foundation of a relationship.

In fact, love isn't just a feeling and an emotion. It's an attitude. It's a mindset. It's the determination to be there for your spouse no matter what (with the exception of infidelity).

It's situations like these that would make many young people of our generation question the necessity of marriage. I still think it's very necessary because it's a sacred covenant made before the Most High. Unfortunately, that covenant is reduced to a status. They can keep the status. I'll hold onto its sacredness.

Looking back, before I got locked up, I must say, I do miss having Jafari around as a younger brother. He was full of such potential. I hope he has peace wherever he is.

Chapter 2

Haze isn't the same. His new friends aren't the best company for him. They seem to have brought out his darker side. A darker side I wouldn't imagine. It's because of that why I wasn't too fond of him hanging around Jafari.

I have to wonder if you could really ever know someone through and through. People change and not always for the better. Then I'll know it's my time to distance myself. When I found out the type of company he was keeping, I wasn't surprised to learn that he stopped taking lessons from Jeonsa. I think my absence had a lot to do with his decision to drop out.

After Jafari's funeral, I caught up with Grandma. She told me he didn't really follow the rules, he skipped school a lot and got into fights. Cooking seemed to be the only thing that Jafari found peace in. He was even considering the Culinary Arts program once he graduated.

Regarding Dad's murder, Grandma told me that Winston turned himself and his accomplices in for robbing and trying to kill Dad. She even told me that Winston ended up getting murdered not too long after getting into prison. I think he got murdered for informing the police. What's good is that justice has been served and that Dad's death wasn't in vain.

I don't know why when we grow up, we refer to the past as the good old days but I do miss him.

Dad was such an inspiration. I just feel like he undermined the value of what he built with Mom. I wish he didn't fall prey to the fickle seduction of another woman. What's done in the darkness always comes to light.

I understand he felt like he couldn't trust Mom anymore. She was deceptive about how she went about the fraud. However, it shouldn't have been an excuse to step out on her like that.

I guess I will never understand why Dad went looking for solace in another woman's arms. I do know that honouring vows when nobody's watching is the measure of true loyalty.

The circumstances of his death taught me to never leave eighty percent for twenty percent. Who would have thought that he'd lose his life to the very woman he viewed as an escape?

Jafari. I miss him too. The police claim they're doing an investigation to find out if the drive-by shooting was targeted. I feel like if I never got locked up, Jafari would probably still be alive today. I guess I'll never really know.

Now, it's literally just me and Mom. They must really want me to lose my cool because too many negative events have taken place within a short period of time. In the midst of it all, I'll turn to the Most High. After all, as my grandmother would say, "We're just passing through. This life is temporary. Do what you came here to do. Leave in peace if you can."

Friends. I don't like that word. Why? Because it ends with, 'END.' English is a funny language. It's a forked tongue.

Haze was like blood. We agreed to not let females get in between us. He broke that, not me. If we were as tight as I thought we were, why couldn't he come speak to me man-to-man?

It's sad to see Haze take the route that he did. I also think the abusive relationship with his father contributed to his delinquent behaviour. If that is the case, I could probably understand that but why drag Jafari and then Naomi into the mix?

Even Jeonsa did his best to ease the situation but Haze stopped going for training altogether. Jeonsa's reasoning for no longer reaching out to Haze was that you can't help those who refuse to receive it.

I have so much love for the people who support me in my life. Unfortunately, people change and not always for the better. That's when my defences go up and I begin to feel like I have to protect myself. Extortion is an understatement. I got hoodwinked.

They say, "if you can't catch Harry, catch his t-shirt." I wonder why Haze and his accomplice were brave enough to view my wife as the t-shirt. It was August 2010 that my friend turned enemy, decided to hold my beloved, Naomi, hostage against her own will. Tupac was right: trust nobody because even his closest friends turned on him.

I don't know who was feeling it more: me or Mom. She wept at the news of Naomi getting kidnapped as if it were her own daughter. God knows what else they're doing to her. I won't even let my mind imagine the possibilities. Not being able to protect and ensure the safety of my wife is one thing but seeing Mom in pain didn't make it any better.

It's been a week since my wife's been gone. We received a phone call from Haze, mocking our family and letting us know he was in Montreal with Naomi. With Dad and Jafari gone, this definitely helped slow down the healing process. To tame the lion within, I took my frustrations out on the basketball court.

Naomi's perfume scent perforated my bedroom. Everything I inhaled, it was like she was right beside me. If anything ever happened to her, I don't think I would re-marry. She's one of a kind. No one else will do. I was thrilled that she didn't mind that I lived with Mom. Well, it only made sense since Naomi and Mom got along so well. I wouldn't have it any other way. Plus, I would be able to save more money and enjoy more fruits of my labor.

She may not be my first but I'm glad we crossed paths. Naomi was worth the wait. Besides basketball, I turned to meditation. I needed to clear my mind before I felt like I was going to lose it.

Chapter 3

As I hopped on the Bloor-Danforth subway line, there she was. I never thought I would see her again. It was Renee. Man. Honestly? I wish I could dodge her because I don't feel for small talk right now. She spotted me before I could reposition myself.

"It's been too long. Don't you think?" Renee seductively whispered. I didn't respond but shorty was looking nice though. No lie. I saw the lust in her eyes. Naomi being my wife didn't phase her.

"I really wanted to do more than just dance with you the other night." I still said nothing.

"I wasn't sure if you were feeling me like that."

She got nerve yo. I wasn't feeling her and didn't want to tell her. Might hurt her feelings. I'm putting up a resistance. God's gonna work it out.

Chapter 4

After playing some ball, I went to go do some training. I was hoping nobody would be there.

On my way, I saw this quote on the TTC that said *He who angers, conquers you* by Elizabeth Kenny. It made me wonder how much power I was giving to Haze while he held my wife hostage.

I've lost many battles but I can't lose this war. I'm trying to maintain my integrity while doing so. Truthfully? I want him dead right now.

"Come with me to Montreal," I said, teasing Mom. "After buying your brother, I need rest. Go get my daughter-in-law. I'll stay with Grandma and look after the barbershop for you." Mom is dope.

I Googled the cheapest ticket to Montreal and booked a one-way ticket and a room at Hotel Le Dauphin Montreal Centre-Ville on 400 rue Marais in Quebec City.

I had less than 24 hours to spear. I headed to the basketball court and I just had to bump into Renee. Again.

"Seriously, We keep bumping into each other. I wonder if this is a sign," Renee stated.

"Not even," I shut it down.

"You don't have to be so dry you know. You already know how I feel about you."

"Yea. I know but I can't mess with you on that level. You don't even know me like that," I told her.

"Let me know what I need to do to make it right"

"You're fine just the way you are. Just not for me."

"There's got to be some sort of possibility."

"You sound like a hopeless romantic."

"Maybe"

"Besides. I don't know that I'm the only man you're digging. I'm expendable."

"I love the companionship of a man. I find it hard to be alone."

"I hear you but you have to be able to enjoy your own company and be your own best friend before you go seeking the companionship of another man."

"A woman can only do so much by herself. I can't marry myself. I can't breed myself."

"It's not that simple."

"I love my wife. I gotta go though."

I had to leave it at that. Too much on my dome. I hope Renee gets better at loving herself.

Chapter 5

I took a quick half-hour nap and one of the coldest showers to kill whatever lust stirred up after bumping into Renee.

After packing my bag, I boarded Porter Airlines flight 777. Everything went as planned. I got the window seat. Rubbed the scuff I had on my J's. I was rocking the red and black 5's.

The plane took off. I was looking forward to getting my wife back.

"Would you like a snack?" the male flight attendant politely asked.

"No. Thanks," I replied. I just wanted to bump some Tupac until I landed.

Anxiety grew. Time was crawling. The pilot makes his announcement.

"We are 10 minutes away from Montreal-Pierre Elliot Trudeau International Airport. The time in Montreal is now 10pm. Your designated flight attendant will gather your trays and any waste that needs to be disposed of. Please keep your area neat and tidy. We will land at ten, ten pm. Please complete your customs documentation your flight attendant will give you to fill out shortly."

As soon as I got my bags, I called Mom.

"Hey, Son!" she said in excitement.

"Hey, Mom. I just reached."

"Alright. Be safe. Call me if you need anything."

"Ok. Love you."

"I love you too Isaiah."

I set my alarm for seven am the next morning. I got a call at 9:30am from a funny number. It was Naomi on the other line. She got away and was at Parc Jean-Drapeau. I dipped so quick to go meet up with her. I hopped in the next taxi and got there within, like, twenty minutes. I got out and was relieved. She was untouched. Beautiful. Whole.

I couldn't stop holding her when we were in the taxi heading back to the hotel.

When when we got back, I put it on her. Kissing her neck. Putting my hand down her lotus flower balm. I felt Niagara Falls through my fingers. Then, I started kissing her back. I could hear her heavy breathing. A little moaning here and there. Squeezed her breasts from behind and then went inside her. Deep. She gripping me now. I bust a milky way in her galaxy after only four strokes. I kept going though because I was still so hard. I gave her more passion marks than Cupid's supply of arrows. Endless. I turned her over to ride me. I love when she rides me. Grip my chest. Hold me in her arms while she whispers sweet everything in my ears. After that, I spooned her. She kept coming. Three hours later, I bust the biggest nut. I stayed inside her until my erection was fully gone. I really missed my pussy.

I woke up the next morning to go grab some breakfast. I didn't want to wake her up because she looked so peaceful.

Why did I come back and see that the window was broken? No Naomi in sight. This gotta be a sick joke or something. How the hell did they know where to find her?! I'm about to be a mad man right now!

Chapter 6

My phone rang three hours later. It felt like an eternity.

"You want your woman back? Be at the blue building by the same park you picked her up from in 2 hours," Haze demanded.

This is past ridiculous.

I bought a 9mm handgun and rented a car for the meet-up. The building looked like something out of an action movie: abandoned and run down.

10 minutes upon arrival, a black 2015 Mercedes-Benz C250 pulled up. Haze and his minion exited the car first. I exited my car and got heated when I saw my wife getting manhandled. She had duct tape around her mouth.

They entered the building and I wasted no time following right behind them. The doors were vandalized, rats everywhere and the lights were so dim that I had to use the flashlight on my phone to guide my path. They took her into this room with no door and a broken window.

"I see you made it on time," said Haze. I said nothing.

I stared at Naomi and could see the despair in her eyes. One of her eyes was black. The way I wanted to bust a cap in both their asses. But I kept my cool because I didn't want to put her in any more danger.

"Are you serious? Why you messing with what's mine?!" I said.

"I'm dead serious. Don't get loud with me," he replies and then starts his evil laugh.

"Why are you doing this?"

"You really wanna know?"!

"Yeah, man. This has nothing to do with - "

"Shut the fuck up man! Renee. Renee! You been messing with my woman. She told me she was pregnant and got an abortion. She said she didn't know who the father was. Like fuck man. You get all the bitches. Why you gotta mess with mines?"

"I never slept with Renee. Baby, don't listen to him."

"How would you feel if I sexed your wife?"

"Listen Haze. Renee ain't your wife. With all due respect, there's no comparison."

"You were my best friend Isaiah. You broke the code!"

I signalled Naomi to kick the minion that was holding her, in the nuts. Haze lit his cigarette and that was my only chance to execute.

I shot Haze in the leg and his accomplice twice in the torso. I was able to remove the duct tape from my wife's mouth. I gave her the keys to the whip. I didn't want her to see me finish them.

"Go to hell!" Haze said in excruciating pain.

"After you," I said. I bust a cap right in his head. I watched him bleed to death. I wanted to make sure he wasn't alive. I closed his eyes and broke down at the same time. It hurt to kill my once best friend. Oh yea: I also finished his minion. I couldn't take any chances.

We bought tickets from Montreal-Pierre Elliot Trudeau International Airport.

"I never slept with Renee," I told Naomi.

"I know baby. Haze is a sick man. I thought I was never going to see you again. I thought he was going to rape me. Instead, he gave this black eye for trying to leave the first time. They were able to track me down because they slipped a tracker in my clothes while I was asleep. That's why they were able to capture me at the hotel. I wish the hotel had a working alarm system."

I held her in my arms. We sat and waited for twenty minutes before boarding the plane. I defied the odds.